HOW TO TRAP a Leprechaun

Written by Sue Fliess
Illustrated by Emma Randall

Sky Pony Press • New York

Legend tells of tiny elves
who visit once a year.

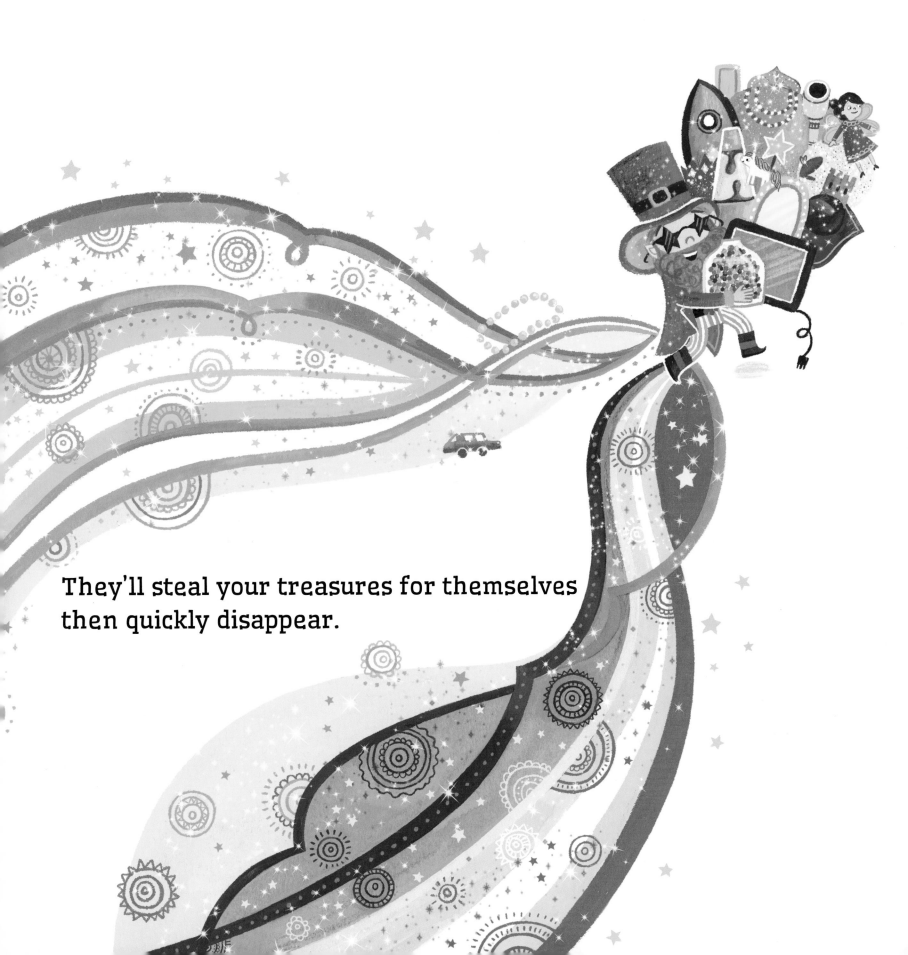

They'll steal your treasures for themselves
then quickly disappear.

If you catch a leprechaun,
he'll grant a wish, I'm told.

But if he gets away, too bad—
no wish, no luck, no gold!

POOF!

Small and full
of trickery,

TRICKERY LEVEL

they'll fool you if they can.

I think
I GOT
HIM!

Catching one takes smarts and skill—
but most of all, a plan.

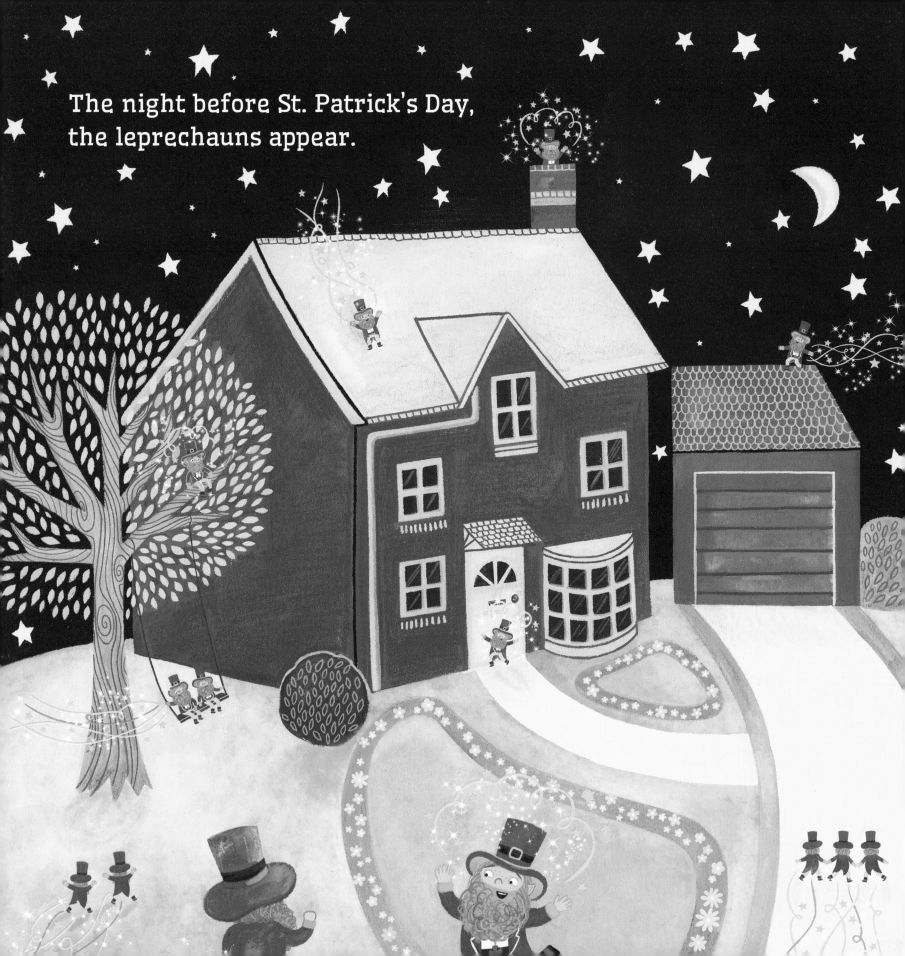

The night before St. Patrick's Day,
the leprechauns appear.

If you wish to capture one,

you'll need the proper gear.

First, you'll need to build a trap—
one he can't escape.

Grab a box,

a bottle cap,

some glitter,

glue,

and tape.

Use gold paint to coat the rocks.
He will think they're real.

Scatter them inside the box
and he will come to steal!

Pour some glue inside the box
and build a rainbow slide.

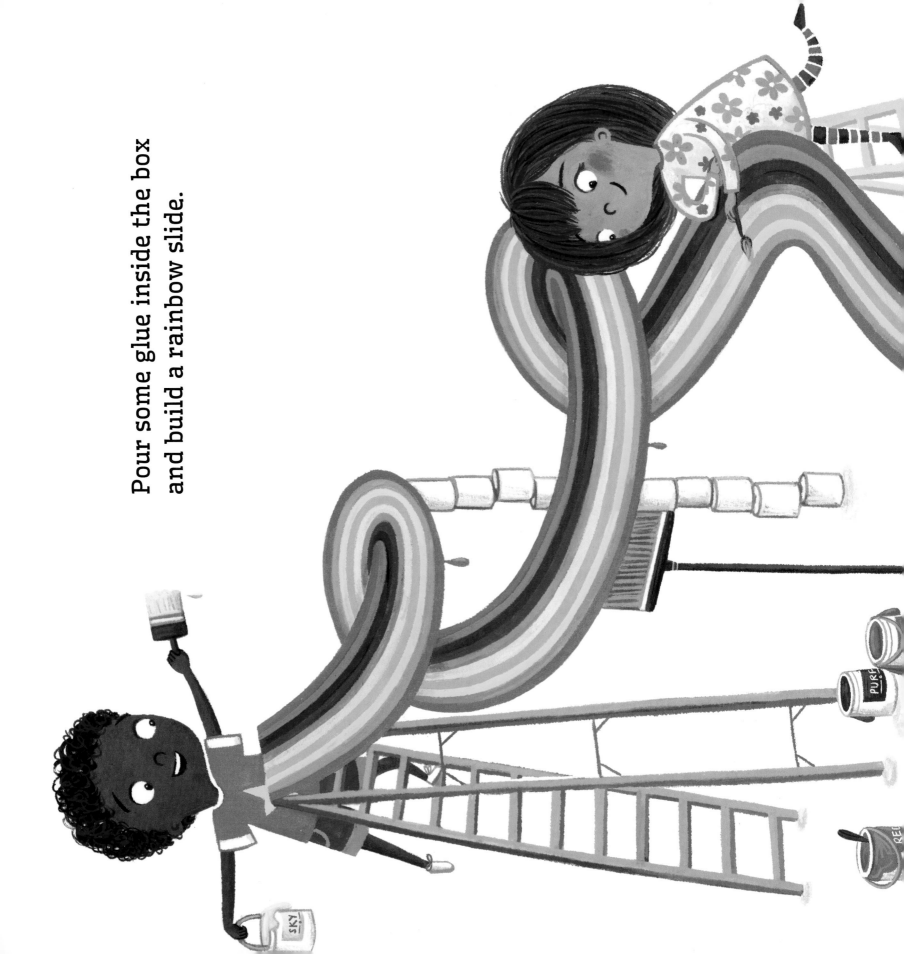

He'll take a ride
to find the gold—
but find he's stuck
inside!

Leprechauns come out at night

so they can sneak around.

Now close the drapes and dim the light
and wait without a sound . . .

Did you hear that?

CRINKLE!

Snap!

Quickly, check your snare.

Shucks! He just escaped the trap!
He could be anywhere!

Look at this! He left his shoe—

and in the shoe a note.

Tiny words . . . addressed to you!
And this is what he wrote:

It's a shame he got away.
But please don't shed a tear.

Go enjoy St. Patrick's Day,
and try again next year!

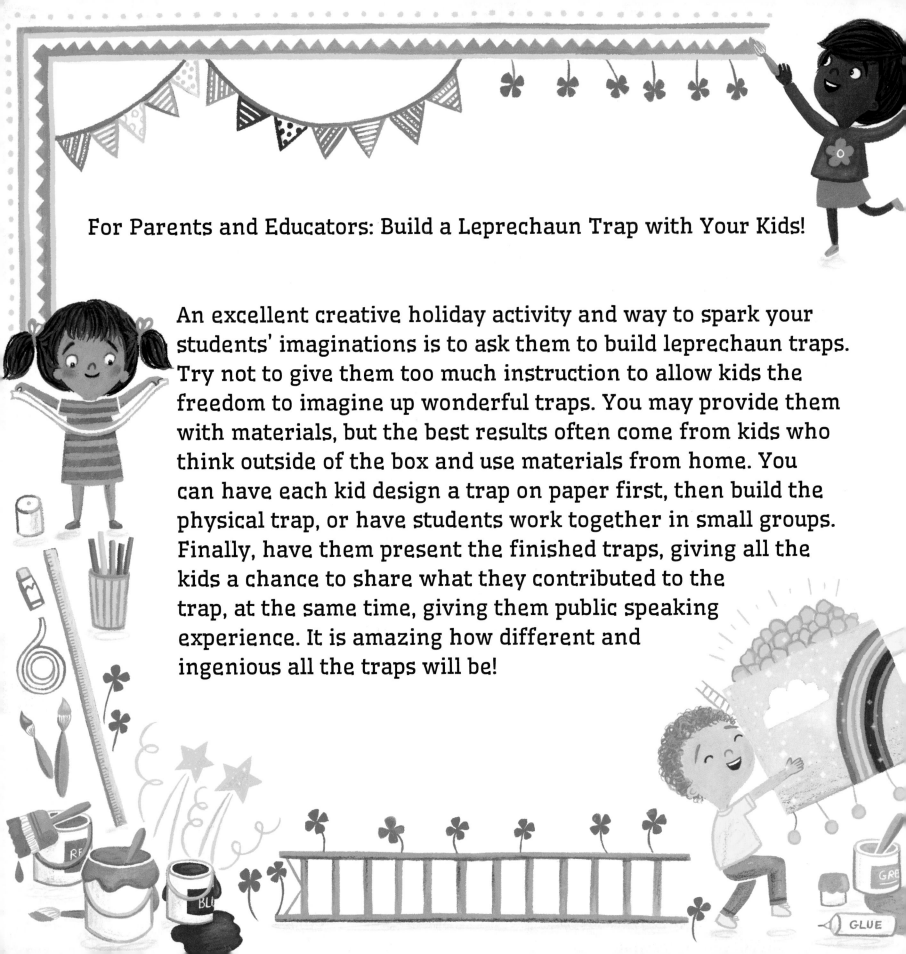

For Parents and Educators: Build a Leprechaun Trap with Your Kids!

An excellent creative holiday activity and way to spark your students' imaginations is to ask them to build leprechaun traps. Try not to give them too much instruction to allow kids the freedom to imagine up wonderful traps. You may provide them with materials, but the best results often come from kids who think outside of the box and use materials from home. You can have each kid design a trap on paper first, then build the physical trap, or have students work together in small groups. Finally, have them present the finished traps, giving all the kids a chance to share what they contributed to the trap, at the same time, giving them public speaking experience. It is amazing how different and ingenious all the traps will be!

You may wish to talk to your kids about leprechauns and Irish folklore before having them build a trap, so they have some knowledge of leprechauns and a sense of what to put in their traps.

A few quick notes: leprechauns are Irish elves that take the form of miniature men. They are clever, magical shoemakers that enjoy creating mischief, pulling pranks, and making jokes. They like gold, coins, or shiny, sparkly objects, and often steal or "borrow" things—usually under cover of darkness. Folklore states that if you do see a leprechaun, you should keep your eyes on him at all times. Evidently, the second you look away, he may disappear. Leprechauns are also known to love rainbows, because as legend has it, a pot of gold can be found at the end of a rainbow. Are you clever enough to find the end of the rainbow?

Happy trapping!

Sky Pony Press books may be purchased in bulk at special discounts for sales promotion, corporate gifts, fund-raising, or educational purposes. Special editions can also be created to specifications. For details, contact the Special Sales Department, Sky Pony Press, 307 West 36th Street, 11th Floor, New York, NY 10018 or info@skyhorsepublishing.com.

Sky Pony® is a registered trademark of Skyhorse Publishing, Inc.®, a Delaware corporation.

Visit our website at www.skyponypress.com.

10 9 8 7 6 5

Manufactured in the United States of America, March 2019
This product conforms to CPSIA 2008

Library of Congress Cataloging-in-Publication Data is available on file.

Cover design and illustrations by Emma Randall

Print ISBN: 978-1-5107-0670-5
Ebook ISBN: 978-1-5107-0671-2